Buzz and Bi
in the
Monster
Maze

Hello, I'm Buzz and this is Bingo!

Woof!

Written by Alan Durant

Illustrated by Sholto Walker

 Collins

One night, Buzz and Bingo
were walking in the forest.
They came to a sign that said:
"This way to the Monster Party."

Under it, in smaller letters, it said:
"To get to the Monster Party,
you must find your way through
the Monster Maze."

2

"A Monster Maze!" said Buzz. "We're not afraid, are we, Bingo? And we *love* parties."

"Woof," said Bingo, very quietly. He didn't like the sound of monsters at all.

"There's a full moon, so we'll be able to see where we're going," said Buzz. "Come on, Bingo."

Buzz walked into the Monster Maze and Bingo hid behind him.

They hadn't got very far when something flapped in front of them. It was a man in a black cape. He had a white face, red eyes and two very sharp fangs. Bingo shivered.

"Wow! Fangtastic!" said Buzz. "You must be Dracula."

"*Count* Dracula," the man said. "Who are you?"

"I'm Buzz and this is Bingo," said Buzz. "We're trying to find our way to the Monster Party."

"So am I," said Count Dracula. "But I'm lost in this Monster Maze."

"Well, come with us," said Buzz. "We'll find the way out together."

Buzz, Bingo and Dracula hadn't gone much further when they heard a horrible howling.
"What *is* that terrible noise?" groaned Dracula.

When they turned the corner, they saw a hairy beast howling at the moon. Bingo started howling, too.

"Who are you?" Buzz asked, when at last it was quiet.

"My name is Howling Wolf," sobbed the beast.

"I'm a werewolf."

"Why are you crying?" asked Buzz.

"I have to sing at the Monster Party and I'm lost
in this maze," sighed Howling Wolf.

8

"Please don't cry," said Buzz. "I'm Buzz, this is Bingo
and this is *Count* Dracula. We're going to the Monster
Party, too. We'll help you find your way out of
this maze."
"Oh, thank you," said Howling Wolf, dabbing his eyes.

Buzz, Bingo, Count Dracula and Howling Wolf walked up one path and down another …

… and another …

… and another.

Oof! Something bumped into Dracula and knocked him over.

"Ow!" cried an angry voice.

It was a troll with the longest nose that Buzz had ever seen.

"That's the fifth time I've bumped my nose in this stupid maze," growled the troll.

"At this rate I'll never get to the Monster Party."

"Perhaps we can help," said Buzz. "My name's Buzz, this is Bingo, this is Count Dracula and this is Howling Wolf. We're going to the Monster Party, too. Why don't you come with us?"

So the troll joined Buzz, Bingo, Dracula and
Howling Wolf in the Monster Maze.
They walked for a long time but couldn't find
the way out.
"I think we're going round in circles," said Buzz.

Suddenly Bingo started barking.
"Look," said the troll, "I think your dog's found something."
Bingo was pulling at something long and white. It was caught on a bush and there was lots more of it along the path.

"It's a bandage," said Buzz. "I wonder where that came from?"

"I think it's Mummy's," said Howling Wolf.

"Has your mummy cut herself?" asked Buzz.

Dracula licked his lips.

"It's not my mummy," said Howling Wolf.

"It's just Mummy. And he's a man."

"A man called Mummy?" said the troll, puzzled.

"He means a mummy from Ancient Egypt," laughed Buzz.

He had an idea. "If we follow this bandage,
it might lead us out of the maze," he said.
"And we won't keep going down the same path.
Well done, Bingo!"

"Woof!" woofed Bingo happily – and he was off.
"Come on, let's follow him," said Buzz.

At last Bingo, Buzz, Dracula, Howling Wolf and the troll got out of the Monster Maze.
"Look, there's Mummy!" said Howling Wolf. "He's going to need a new bandage when he gets to the party."

17

Dracula, Howling Wolf and the troll thanked Buzz and Bingo for helping them to find their way out of the maze.

"You must come with us to the Monster Party," they said. "You can meet our friends!"

At the Monster Party there were monsters of every kind. There was a hobgoblin, a yeti, a dog with three heads and a gorgon with snakes in her hair. Buzz thought he saw the Loch Ness Monster, but he wasn't sure.

Howling Wolf was happy at last. He sang with his Silver Bullet Band. They played the Monster Stomp and everybody danced.

"Wow," said Buzz, "this is really *monstrous!* I *love* this music, don't you, Bingo?"

But Bingo didn't care about the music or the dancing.
He had found something that he liked much more –
a monstrous bone!

✿ Ideas for guided reading ✿

Learning objectives: Prepare and retell stories, using dialogue and narrative from text; identify and describe characters; discriminate orally syllables in multi-syllabic words; consider mood and atmosphere in a live or recorded performance.

Curriculum links: Citizenship: Choices

Interest words: Count Dracula, werewolf, monster, Howling Wolf, troll, mummy

Word count: 780

Resources: whiteboard and pens, tape recorder, classroom instruments

Getting started

This book can be read over two sessions.

- Show the children the book and discuss the title and cover. Read the blurb and ask them to predict what the story will be about.

- Ask the children to name monsters they know of and draw up a list on the whiteboard. Practise reading these and counting syllables, e.g. *mon/ster, were/wolf.*
- Walk through the book up to p21 and discuss who Buzz and Bingo meet, and ask the children to predict at different points what might happen in the story.

Reading and responding

- Ask the children to read up to p21 independently and silently. Listen to each child reading a short passage aloud, and prompt and praise for fluency, using cues to work out unfamiliar words and self-correction.
- As they are reading ask the children to consider: *Who was frightened in the story? How do you know? Why is the story funny? Are the monsters scary? Why not?*
- Look at the story map on pp22-23 and ask the children to recount what happened in the maze using the points on the map to help.